CONTEI

D1352307

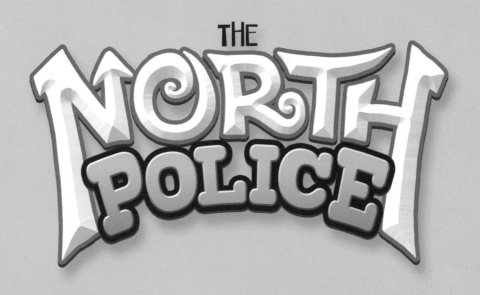

THE NORTH POLICE

The North Police are

the elves who solve crimes

at the North Pole.

These are their stories...

CHAPTER 1

Red-nosed reindeer

It was a bright, cold morning in Christmas Town.

In the North Police station, the chief shouted, "Detectives Sprinkles and Sugarplum! Get into my office! Now!"

Sitting beside the chief was an unhappy reindeer. He had a shiny red nose.

"What's happened to your nose?" asked Sugarplum.

GLOSSARY

badge small piece of metal pinned to a police officer's uniform: the badge tells people that the police officer is an official member of the police force

detective someone who investigates crimes

disguise costume worn to hide what someone really looks like

handcuffs metal rings joined by a chain that are locked around a criminal's wrists to stop them escaping

suspect someone thought to be involved in a crime

These are their stories...

only from RAINTREE!

AUTHOR

Scott Sonneborn has written many books, a circus (for Ringling Bros. Barnum & Bailey) and lots of TV programmes. He's been nominated for one Emmy and spent three amazing years working at DC Comics. He lives in Los Angeles, USA, with his wife and their two sons.

ILLUSTRATOR

Omar Lozano lives in Monterrey, Mexico. He has always been crazy about illustration, constantly on the lookout for awesome things to draw. In his spare time, he watches lots of films, reads fantasy and sci-fi books and draws! Omar has worked for Marvel, DC, IDW, Capstone and many other publishers.